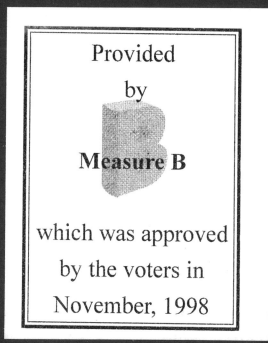

A Hanukkah Treasury

A Hanukkah

T·R·E·A·S·U·R·Y

Edited by Eric A. Kimmel

Illustrated by Emily Lisker

· · · · · ·

Henry Holt and Company · New York

Henry Holt and Company, Inc., *Publishers since 1866*, 115 West 18th Street, New York, New York 10011

Henry Holt is a registered trademark of Henry Holt and Company, Inc.

Compilation copyright © 1998 by Eric A. Kimmel. Illustrations copyright © 1998 by Emily Lisker. All rights reserved.
Published in Canada by Fitzhenry & Whiteside Ltd., 195 Allstate Parkway, Markham, Ontario L3R 4T8

Library of Congress Cataloging-in-Publication Data
A Hanukkah treasury / by Eric Kimmel; illustrated by Emily Lisker.
p.   cm.
Summary: Presents stories, songs, recipes, and activities related to the celebration of Hanukkah.
1. Hanukkah—Juvenile literature.   [1. Hanukkah.]   I. Kimmel, Eric A.   II. Lisker, Emily, ill.
BM695.H3H39   1997   296.4'35—dc21   97-24428

ISBN 0-8050-5293-3   First Edition—1998   Typography by Meredith Baldwin
Printed in Italy. 10 9 8 7 6 5 4 3 2 1

The artist used acrylic paints on canvas to create the illustrations for this book.

To Aydan, Akiva, Maytal, and Zakai
—E. A. K.

To Bill Calhoun
—E. L.

Contents

A Hanukkah Treasury

Hanukkah, O Hanukkah!

(Traditional)

Hanukkah, O Hanukkah! A festival of joy.
A jolly day, a holiday for every girl and boy.
Set the dreidels spinning, all week long.
Taste the sizzling latkes. Sing the ancient songs.
And while we're rejoicing,
The candles are burning low.
One for each night, they shine clear and bright
To remind us of days long ago.
Telling the story, how God—Praise His Glory!—
Brought triumph in days long ago.

Festival of Lights

Eric A. Kimmel

Hanukkah, O Hanukkah! Is there anything like it? The Festival of Lights is a joyous holiday. Candles flicker; dreidels spin; latkes sizzle in the pan as Jewish people the world over recall the heroes of ancient times and celebrate their mighty deeds.

Hanukkah is unique in many ways. Although it ranks as a minor festival, it is one of the most beloved holidays in the Jewish year. It lasts eight days, as long as the major feasts of Sukkot, Pesach, and Shavuot. However, there is no special synagogue service for Hanukkah. The holiday is largely celebrated at home. And although Hanukkah certainly is a religious holiday, it is traditionally observed by playing children's games.

Hanukkah is the only significant Jewish holiday not mentioned in the Bible. The original Hebrew texts related to Hanukkah have been lost. Nearly everything known about the Maccabees and their struggle against the Greek king Antiochus comes from a collection of writings called the Apochrypha and the work of a later Jewish historian named Flavius Josephus. Without these Greek texts, we would know very little about Hanukkah's origins.

All these contradictions make Hanukkah a holiday like no other. What is it all about? What does Hanukkah really mean?

The essence of Hanukkah is simple. It celebrates events that occurred more than two thousand years ago, when a tiny band of heroes, armed with little more than their faith in God, defeated a mighty empire and proved to the world that miracles truly happen to those with the courage to believe in them.

The Story of the Maccabees

Eric A. Kimmel

Once there was a king. His name was Antiochus. He ruled a vast empire that stretched from the borders of Egypt to the mountains of Persia. People from dozens of different nations resided within its boundaries: Babylonians, Arabs, Persians, Medes, Syrians, Jews, and Greeks, as well as others whose names have been forgotten.

Antiochus was a Greek, the descendant of one of Alexander the Great's generals. When Alexander's empire broke apart after his death, the leaders of his army seized kingdoms for themselves. They and their descendants fought and plotted against each other. Antiochus had many enemies, and none of them ruled a nation as divided as his. His subjects spoke different languages and worshiped different gods. Surely they would prefer to rule themselves, Antiochus reasoned. If his enemies could encourage his subjects to rebel, his kingdom would be shattered.

But what if, instead of numerous gods, languages, and cultures, his subjects had only one? What if they were all Greeks? A united Greek kingdom would be so powerful that no enemy could hope to defeat it.

Antiochus set out to turn his subjects into Greeks. It was less difficult than expected, for the process had been going on since the days of Alexander. The Greeks possessed a great culture, admired by people all over the ancient world. They worshiped beauty and wisdom. If a person learned to speak Greek, took a Greek name, dressed as a Greek, sacrificed to Greek gods, and lived in a Greek city, he almost always gained wealth and power. Within a few generations people forgot that their ancestors had been Phoenicians, Babylonians, or Elamites. They came to consider themselves Greeks.

Antiochus's plan succeeded beyond expectation. Greek colonies blossomed all over his empire. He didn't have to use force. The most intelligent and ambitious people in his realm flocked to become part of the worldwide civilization represented by the culture of Greece.

In only one place was there trouble: Judea, a small province bordering Egypt. The Judeans, or Jews, as they came to be called, were a peculiar people. Descendants of ancient Israelites whom Moses led out of slavery, they worshiped an invisible god whom they believed created the universe out of nothing. This god had no brothers or sisters; no wife or children. He had no statue or image because He had no shape or form. He was not only the god of Judea; He ruled over the entire world. All other gods, even the beautiful deities of Greece, were false.

The Jews did not oppose everything the Greeks had to offer. They admired the democratic way by which Greek cities governed themselves. They recognized the wisdom of Greek philosophers. They saw the advantage of one universal language spoken by people all over the world. However, they refused to change their religion. The gods of Greece would never replace the God of Israel.

Antiochus decided to use force against the Jews. If one small people could resist his will, so might others. He sent an army to occupy Jerusalem, Judea's capital. Greek soldiers seized the Temple, the sacred shrine of the God of Israel. They erected a statue of Zeus and slaughtered pigs and other unclean animals on the ancient altar as offerings to the gods of Greece. Armed companies spread through the countryside, setting up shrines to Greek gods in every town and inviting people to worship.

One day soldiers came to the village of Modi'in. A Jewish man who had become a Greek sacrificed a pig. He called upon his fellow Jews to show their loyalty to the king by joining him in worshiping Zeus. One old man stepped forward. He was Mattathias, a respected priest of the Hasmonean family. Without warning, Mattathias drew a sword and struck the traitor down. His five strong sons attacked the soldiers. Led by Mattathias and his family, the people of Modi'in wiped out the Greeks. Then they fled to the hills, calling on all who believed in the God of Israel to join them.

Antiochus sent soldiers to punish the rebels. Mattathias's small

band could not hope to defeat a Greek army. Instead, they used surprise tactics. The Jews ambushed the Greeks, staged sudden raids, cut off their patrols.

When Mattathias died, his son Judah took over as commander. Judah excelled at guerrilla warfare. His followers called him "Maccabee." No one is sure what this word originally meant. The most accepted view is that it means "Hammerer," after the way Judah hammered the Greek forces sent against him.

A Greek general named Gorgias thought he knew how to fight guerrillas. He led his main force through the hills for a surprise attack on Judah's camp. But Judah outsmarted him. While Gorgias was away from his own base, searching for the Maccabees, Judah circled around and struck the undefended Greek camp at a place called Emmaus. Gorgias returned from his night march to find his tents in flames, his animals driven off, and his supplies burned. He had to retreat without catching sight of Judah and his followers.

Enraged by these failures, Antiochus decided to wipe out the Maccabees once and for all. He gathered an enormous force, complete with war elephants. The Maccabees met the Greeks at a place called Bet Zur. Judah instructed his bowmen and slingers to shoot at the *mahouts,* the men from India who trained and guided the elephants. With their Indian trainers dead or injured, the elephants panicked. They plunged back through the Greek lines, scattering Antiochus's soldiers. The Maccabees charged through the gaps, and won the battle.

The victorious Maccabees entered Jerusalem in November, 164 B.C.E. Judah led his soldiers to the Temple. He found the Temple an empty shell. The ritual objects had been stolen. The altar was polluted with the blood of unclean animals. The Maccabees put aside their weapons. Together with the people of Jerusalem, they worked day and night to remove all traces of idol worship from the Temple.

On the twenty-fifth day of the Hebrew month of Kislev, Judah and his followers rededicated the Temple to the worship of the God of Israel. The ceremonies lasted eight days. This was the first Hanukkah. The word means "dedication."

There is another reason why Hanukkah lasts eight days. According to legend, when the Maccabees prepared to light the menorah, the seven-branched gold candelabrum that stood in the Temple, they discovered that the lamp oil had been spoiled by the Greeks. They found just one small flask whose seal had not been broken. It contained only enough oil to light the menorah for one day. Yet that tiny amount miraculously burned for eight days, long enough for more oil to be brought to Jerusalem.

Ever since that time more than two thousand years ago, Jewish people all over the world have celebrated Hanukkah, the Festival of Lights. As the candles in the menorah burn, they recall the miracle of the tiny flask of oil that burned for eight days, and the even greater miracle of how a tiny band of heroic men and women defeated a mighty empire and won the right to worship God in their own way.

From the First Book of Maccabees

I Maccabees 4:36–61

But Judah said to his brothers: "Now that we have crushed our enemies, let us go up to Jerusalem to cleanse the Temple and rededicate it." So the whole army gathered and went up to Mount Zion. There they found the Temple empty, the altar covered with the blood of unclean animals, the gates burnt down, the courts overgrown like a wooded hillside, and the priests' rooms in ruins. They tore their garments, wailed loudly, put ashes on their heads, and fell on their faces to the ground. They sounded the shofars and cried aloud to Heaven.

Then Judah ordered his troops to keep the Greek army from attacking while he cleansed the Temple. He selected pure priests, holy men devoted to the Torah. They cleansed the Temple, removing the filth that lay everywhere. The priests discussed what to do with the polluted altar and rightly decided to pull it down. However, since these stones had once been holy, they were not thrown away. The priests stored them beneath the Temple Mount until a true prophet should arise to advise what should be done with them. Then the priests took unhewn stones, as the Torah commands, and built a new altar on the model of the previous one. They rebuilt the Temple, restored its interior, and blessed the Temple courts. They restored the sacred vessels and the menorah, and brought the altar of incense and the table into the Temple. They burnt incense on the altar and lit the lamps on the menorah to shine within the Temple. When they had put the loaves of challah bread on the table and hung the curtains, all their work was complete.

Then, early in the morning on the twenty-fifth day of the ninth month, the month Kislev, a sacrifice was offered as the Torah commands on the new altar. On the anniversary of the day the Greeks profaned it, on that same day, it was rededicated, with hymns of thanksgiving, to the music of harps and lutes and cymbals. All the people stretched themselves on the ground, worshiping and praising the God of Israel, Who had given them the victory.

They celebrated the rededication of the altar for eight days. With great rejoicing, the people brought burnt-offerings to the Temple. They sacrificed peace-offerings and thank-offerings. They decorated the front of the Temple with golden wreaths and ornamental shields. They restored the gates and the priests' rooms, and fitted them with doors. The people felt great happiness and joy, because the shameful disgrace done to their Temple and their nation by the Greeks had been washed away.

Then Judah, his brothers, and the whole house of Israel decreed that the rededication of the altar should be observed with joy and celebration at the same time each year, for eight days, beginning on the twenty-fifth of Kislev.

Not by Might, Not by Power*

Lyrics adapted from Zechariah 4:6   Music by Debbie Friedman

*The phrase "Not by might, not by power . . ." comes from the prophet
Zechariah's vision of the menorah. Portions from the Book of
Zechariah are read as part of the Hanukkah Sabbath service.

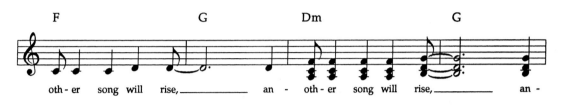

oth - er   song will   rise, _____ an - oth-er   song will rise, _____ an -

oth - er   song _____ will _____ rise. _____

Not _____ by _____ might _____ and _____ not _____ by _____

pow - er _____ but by   spir - it a - lone   shall we all live in _____

peace. _____ peace. _____ Not by   might, _____ not by

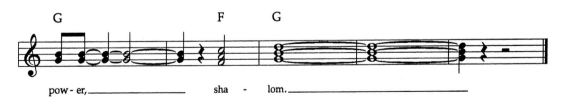

pow - er, _____ sha - lom. _____

15

Holy Lights, Holy Lamps

Eric A. Kimmel

The flickering glow of oil lamps and candles has been part of Jewish worship for centuries. In addition to the lights that are kindled during the eight days of Hanukkah, two candles are lit in every Jewish home on Friday evening to mark the coming of Sabbath. A special braided candle with several wicks is kindled during the Havdalah ceremony on Saturday evening to mark the Sabbath's end. Candles are lit at the beginning of all major holidays and festivals. Many Jewish families light a long-burning *yahrzeit* lamp to mark the anniversary of the death of a family member.

In the synagogue, a *ner tamid,* or "eternal light," hangs above the cabinet containing the Torah scrolls. Every synagogue also contains at least one representation of the seven-branched candlestick called the *menorah.*

The menorah is one of the most ancient and beloved symbols of the Jewish people. The first menorah is described in the Bible. It had six branches, three on each side, curving up from a central stem that stood on a three-legged base. The stem and its branches were ornamented with almond-shaped cups, knobs, and flowers. The flowers held oil-burning lamps.

No one is sure why there were seven branches. Most likely, the menorah represented the universe as people of the time understood it. The central lamp represented the earth. The six branches were the sun and planets that revolved around it.

According to tradition, the menorah was created from one piece of solid gold. God gave Moses precise directions about how to make it. These can be found in the Book of Exodus, but they are not very clear. Moses could not understand them. So God drew a picture of the menorah with fire. Even that was not enough. In the end, God told Moses to put a lump of gold in the forge—and the menorah miraculously emerged!

The menorah stood at the southern end of the Tabernacle, the tent where the Ten Commandments and other holy objects were stored. The priests lit the menorah at dusk. It burned through the night, a visible symbol of God's presence watching over the Israelite camp.

No one knows what became of this original menorah. Perhaps it was one of the ten gold menorahs that stood in Solomon's Temple. Could it have survived the Babylonian destruction of Jerusalem in 586 B.C.E.? Unlikely as this may seem, when the exiles returned from Babylon a hundred years later to rebuild the Temple, they brought a menorah with them.

A gold menorah stood in the Second Temple until 169 B.C.E., when it was stolen by Antiochus, along with the other Temple treasures. When the Maccabees rededicated the Temple in 164, they had to create a new menorah out of iron skewers covered with wood and metal. This makeshift menorah was soon replaced by a splendid one made of gold. It stood in the Temple for nearly a hundred years until the Romans destroyed Jerusalem in 70 C.E.

The Roman general Titus staged a triumphal march through Rome to celebrate his conquest of Judea. The menorah and all the Temple treasures were paraded through the streets as spoils of victory. A magnificent arch, the Arch of Titus, was erected as a memorial. It still stands. On it is a scene of Roman soldiers carrying a seven-branched candlestick. This was the last time the menorah was ever seen. After Titus's triumph, it vanished from history. There are rumors of its appearance in North Africa, Spain, and Constantinople, but what finally happened to it is unknown.

In Jerusalem today, a menorah created by British artist Benno Elkan stands before the Knesset, the parliament of modern Israel. It was given to the Knesset in 1956 by the Parliament of Great Britain—a gift from one of the world's oldest legislatures to one of the youngest.

The Roman Empire is long vanished. The Arch of Titus stands amid ruins. But the menorah is the symbol of the modern State of Israel where Jewish people again live, free and proud in their own land.

Light the menorah, the lamp of liberty! May it shine forever in every country, for every people!

עַם יִשְׂרָאֵל חַי!
The nation of Israel lives!

Hanukkah Lamps

Eric A. Kimmel

The special lamp that is lit during the eight days of Hanukkah is also called a menorah. A better name would be *hanukiyah,* or "Hanukkah lamp," to distinguish it from the seven-branched candelabrum that stood in the Temple. No matter what the lamp is called, it is impossible to imagine celebrating Hanukkah without it. Yet no one really knows how, when, or why a special lamp came to be associated with Hanukkah.

The oldest object that can be identified as a Hanukkah lamp was discovered in a cave near Jerusalem. It was carved from a square piece of limestone. The eight slots carved in the stone were intended to hold olive oil and fiber wicks. The lamp dates from the second century C.E., nearly four hundred years after the first Hanukkah.

No earlier Hanukkah lamps have been found. They may not exist. A five-hundred-year gap separates Judah Maccabee's victory in 164 B.C.E. and any known reference to the custom of lighting a special lamp at Hanukkah. The Books of the Maccabees say nothing about it. Neither does Flavius Josephus, the Jewish historian who wrote during the Roman period. What Josephus does say about Hanukkah is: "From that time forward unto this day we celebrate the Festival, calling it 'Lights.'"

Lamps clearly had some role in the earliest Hanukkah celebrations, but exactly what that was and whether special lamps were used remains unknown.

The first reference to lighting a Hanukkah lamp comes from the Talmud. The volumes of the Talmud discuss every aspect of human life. They are the foundation of Jewish religious law. While discussing the rules for observing the Sabbath, the rabbis also considered the ritual of Hanukkah. They established how the Hanukkah lamp would be lit for ages to come.

The rabbis agreed that Hanukkah lights should be kindled in every Jewish home rather than just in the synagogue. On each night the number of lights should be increased by one. These lights were not to be used for illumination. One could not read or work by them. Their sole purpose was to proclaim God's miracle. What miracle was that? The famous legend about the miraculous jar of oil that burned for eight days appears for the first time, five hundred years after the Maccabees' victory.

Since these holy lights could not be used for any ordinary purpose, one could not be used to kindle the others. Another light, or candle, was lit for this purpose. This is the origin of the *shammash*

candle, was lit for this purpose. This is the origin of the *shammash* candle, which serves and guards the rest. The word means "servant," "caretaker," or "guardian."

Hanukkah lamps were originally displayed outside the home, in a special niche to the left of the doorway. However, as these were easily stolen or vandalized, the rabbis ruled that it was acceptable to hang the lamp inside the house. Hanukkah lamps could now be made of more valuable materials, such as brass, pewter, or silver. A metal plate protected the wall from the flames. This backwall allowed the lamp to be hung from a nail. It also provided space for decoration.

Another type of Hanukkah lamp took the shape of an eight-pointed star. It hung from the ceiling. This type was popular in medieval Germany. An example appears in the famous Sarajevo Haggadah.

Sixteenth-century Polish artisans added legs to the backwall design to create a new type of lamp that looked like a bench. These were decorated with a wide variety of Jewish symbols. Polish craftsmen also created a nine-branched standing menorah for Hanukkah use. One spectacular example on exhibit at the Skirball Cultural

in Poland in the early nineteenth century, this Hanukkah lamp takes the shape of an oak tree. A golden bear is climbing the trunk to get at a honeypot on the lowest branch, unaware of the hunter on the ground aiming his gun. The foliage around the tree conceals images of dogs, rabbits, a squirrel, worms, and a caterpillar. It is unclear what these exquisite figures have to do with Hanukkah, but the lamp is certainly a magnificent example of the silversmith's art.

Today, the variety of Hanukkah lamps is endless. Themes range from Noah's Ark to the Holocaust. But no matter whether it burns candles or oil, whether it is made of stone, clay, bronze, silver, or glass, the Hanukkah lamp is part of an ancient heritage that burns as brightly today as it did in the time of the Maccabees.

Hanukkah Haiku

Erica Silverman

Gray days, long dark nights;
but from our Hanukkah lamp—
light light light light light

The Lost Menorah

Howard Schwartz

Rabbi (or Rebbe) Nachman of Bratslav in Eastern Europe was a great Hasidic teacher of the nineteenth century. A man of deep spiritual gifts, he wrote a number of beautiful stories. Howard Schwartz has retold many of them in his books. This is an original story by Schwartz about Rebbe Nachman.

The silver menorah had been in Reb Nussan's family for four hundred years, and family tradition held that it was even older than that. Needless to say, this menorah was precious in the eyes of Reb Nussan, and so he was clutched with fear when he discovered, on the morning of Erev Hanukkah, that it was missing. How could such a thing happen? Reb Nussan and his wife looked everywhere, but it was not to be found. Then Reb Nussan's wife recalled that a man who had been collecting trash to leave at the dump had come to their house a few days before with a covered wagon. Reb Nussan's wife had filled several sacks with things for him to take away—sacks of the same kind in which the menorah had been stored. Somehow he must have taken the sack with the menorah as well and carried it off to the dump.

When Reb Nussan realized that this was the only explanation, he was devastated, for the menorah must now lie at the bottom of the deep valley that served Bratslav as the town dump. There, he was certain, it would never be found. And when this likely truth sank in, Reb Nussan became dejected. He left the house and sat under a bare tree, sinking into gloom and melancholy.

When Reb Nussan's wife saw how this loss had harmed him, she could not bear it, and she blamed herself. So she went to Reb Nachman in tears and told him all that had taken place. When Reb Nachman heard what she had to say, he left his home at once and came to Reb Nussan, who sat blankly at the foot of the tree. So lost was he in his grief that he did not even notice Reb Nachman standing above him, and he was greatly startled when the Rebbe spoke and said, "Why are you sitting here, Nussan, when it is almost Hanukkah and you do not even have a menorah with which to light the candles?"

When Reb Nussan heard these words, he was so startled, he leaped to his feet in anger, and then he realized it was Reb Nachman who had spoken. But he could not understand why the Rebbe would rub salt in his wounds, and he said, "Why must you remind me of this, Rebbe, at such a moment, when I have sustained such a great loss?" And Reb Nachman said, "Because, Nussan, the menorah cannot be considered lost until someone has searched for it."

"What do you mean, Rebbe?" said Nussan. "Surely you do not think it is possible for it to be found?" "And why not, Nussan?" said Reb Nachman. "If it is possible for the coffin of Joseph to be recovered even though it had sunk to the bottom of the Nile, surely it is possible for this precious menorah to be found. Waste no time brooding, Nussan, for if you do not find it by Hanukkah, then it will surely be lost for good."

28

Now Hanukkah would begin that very day at sunset, and in that valley was piled fifty years of trash. Still, Reb Nussan was suddenly filled with hope and determination, and he took leave of Reb Nachman and hurried off to borrow a horse, so that he could complete the task in time. He made the old horse trot as swiftly as it could, but it was noon by the time he reached the valley where the trash was dumped. He tied the horse to a tree and slowly climbed down the sides of the valley until he reached the bottom. There he was overwhelmed by the vast piles of trash which were spread out as far as his eyes could see. Still, Reb Nussan refused to be discouraged, and he waded into the trash, digging with his bare hands.

Before long, his hands were raw and sore, and he wished he had remembered a shovel, for in his haste he had not brought one. All of a sudden Reb Nussan saw a shovel sticking up from the trash. He rushed to it and pulled it out and was completely astonished to discover that it was not only a shovel, but his own shovel as well, a rusty one that he had once thrown away. Then he knew that the shovel was a sign from heaven that there was still hope, and he continued to dig with confidence and determination.

For three hours he dug and dug, till suddenly he came upon a sack which resembled one of his own. And when he tore it open he was blinded for an instant by the reflection of silver in the sun—for he had found the lost menorah at last. Then, with tears rolling down his face and his clothes filthy from the trash, he held up the undamaged menorah and raised his voice in prayer: *"Shema Yisrael, Adonai Elohanu, Adonai Ehad—Hear O Israel, the Lord our God, the Lord is one."*

Hanukkah Lights

J. Patrick Lewis

Verse: Let the miracle and aura
          Of eight lights from that menorah
          Lit from one small vial of oil
          Call the faithful from their toil.

Chorus: As each house begins its glowing,
          People coming, people going
          Mark a time—the overthrowing,
          The defeat of the invaders.
          People born in every nation
          Celebrate our liberation.

Verses: Let us keep the promise simple:
          To rededicate the Temple
          With a symbol to inspire
          Peace and Freedom—candlefire.

          Let no enemies destroy us
          In a season turning joyous,
          For it's Hanukkah that's bringing
          Children laughing, children singing.

          But let every child remember
          That this festival December,
          So enriching a revival,
          Is a hymn to our survival.

          (Repeat chorus)

The Blessing

Peninnah Schram

The Bible says that the prophet Elijah never died. He was taken up to heaven in a fiery chariot. That is why he sometimes returns to earth to help people in trouble, or to teach them an important lesson—in this case, that a beautiful menorah need not be made out of precious metal. It can be as ordinary as . . . potatoes!

A stranger came to a small town on the fifth night of Hanukkah. It was cold and wintry. The snow had stopped falling. As the stranger walked, his footsteps made a deep impression in the sparkling snow and the crunching sound broke the quietness all around him.

The stranger walked slowly past many houses, looking carefully at each one as he passed by. What was he looking for?

"Aha!" he called out softly, and in the coldness of the air his breath formed a puff of white. "Here is the house I'm looking for." And he stopped at a certain cottage.

It was a tiny house compared to the others in the town. There was nothing to make it stand out, except for . . .

The stranger knocked gently on the door. In a moment, the door opened a crack and behind it stood a woman.

"What do you wish?" asked the woman.

"I am a stranger here in town. And it is a cold wintry night. May I come in to warm myself at your stove?" asked the stranger. "The synagogue is dark and cold because everyone has already left to return to their homes to celebrate Hanukkah."

"Oh yes, yes, come in. It would give me great honor to invite you in to join us in our celebration. To be alone, even in the synagogue, is not right on this night. Come in quickly for the cold is bitter and enters quickly too," responded the woman, with a wave of her arm, offering her hospitality without hesitation.

In the small room that the stranger entered sat five children, three older and two much younger. They were sitting close to the stove. Yes, they were trying to get warm, but there was also a sense of impatience, each one staring at the stove as if to be able to see inside it through the bricks.

"Mama, who is there?" asked the oldest child.

"Mama, Mama, *when* will it be ready?" another child asked.

"When, Mama?" echoed the youngest.

"Right away! Right away!" answered the mama as she welcomed in the stranger, taking his heavy fur-lined black coat and hat while motioning him to come nearer to the stove, and, at the same time, gesturing for the children to make room for the guest.

All the children stared at the guest, thinking to themselves: "Who is this stranger? Why is he here? Who invited him to share our *latke-kugel* when there's hardly enough for us?" The stranger read their thoughts from looking at the children's faces. But the youngest, little Rivkele, didn't have those thoughts. Rather, she was just happy to have more company. She ran over to the guest with open arms calling out, "Tell me a story!"

"In a little while, my little bird," replied the stranger with a smile. And when he smiled, it seemed as if his long white beard grew twice as wide and formed many shapes.

In the meantime, the mama had opened the oven and the room was instantly filled with a delicious aroma of a large baked potato latke—almost like a *kugel*—all brown and crisp. Mama took the *latke-kugel* carefully out of the oven with a long wooden-handled paddle and placed it on the table. The children gathered around the table, eyeing this favorite food served especially on Hanukkah, reaching out with their hands as if to touch the pan—miming as if to scoop the whole *latke-kugel* into their mouths—the littler ones imitating the bigger ones.

Actually that *latke-kugel* was big enough for three, maybe four, people, to eat. And now it would have to be divided into seven portions.

The mama found her place at the table, again remembering to welcome the stranger to the Hanukkah table. First came the blessing, which the children wanted to recite quickly, but the mama said it very slowly and the children had to slow down. All this time, the stranger watched each one in turn, smiling mysteriously.

Finally, the mama began to cut the potato *latke-kugel,* dividing most of it equally, except for one piece that was bigger than the rest, and one especially smaller. Each child hoped the biggest piece would "fall" into his or her plate, but it was the stranger, the guest, who was served first and with the biggest piece of the *latke-kugel.* Now the children hoped that they would not "win" the smallest piece, but mama saved that one for herself. Most of the children ate the *latke-kugel* slowly, trying to make it last as long as possible, but some ate it quickly, hoping that somehow more would appear. After eating, they sang some Hanukkah songs while they cleared the table. Then one of the children got the dreidel to play. The others brought some nuts to the table and the dreidel game began.

After a while, Rivkele turned her attention again to the guest and asked, "Can you tell me a story now?"

"Gladly," replied the guest. "But first let me tell you why I came to this house. As you see, I am a stranger in this town. And arriving too late to go to *shul,* I went searching for a Jewish home. Well, on Hanukkah, I knew I could recognize a Jewish home by the

36

menorah in the window. When I saw your beautiful menorah, I knew this was the house I wanted to visit during my stay here in your town."

"Beautiful? It's not even a menorah! It's—potatoes! A potato menorah!" cried out the oldest child, not hiding his shame.

"It's all we have," replied the mama. "We cannot afford to buy a real menorah made of metal. Maybe next year . . ." and her voice faded away. The stranger saw a tear fall on her open hand as if she had held it there—open—in midair just to catch her tear.

"But that is why I came here to this house," continued the stranger. "This is a menorah as real as any other made of silver or gold. It fulfills the *mitzvah* of burning oil with a wick to celebrate our *yom tov*—but it is a menorah filled also with love of *mitzvah*. When you have money, then it's easy to buy a menorah. But you and your mama had to make your menorah. You chose the potatoes with great care. You cut open the potatoes carefully. You counted how many halves you needed for five wicks and a *shammash*. And you put them in the window for the world to see. *Nu?* What can be more beautiful than that?" Then turning to the youngest children, he said, "So now, little ones, I will tell you a story of wonder and light."

And the stranger sat near the stove with the children and the mama around him and told the story of the Maccabees and their fight for freedom and how they found and lit the cruse of oil in the restored menorah to dedicate the Temple in Jerusalem. And how a miracle happened when the little bit of oil, enough for only one night, lasted for eight nights.

When the stranger had finished the story, he added, "And since this is the fifth night of Hanukkah, it is a tradition to give Hanukkah *gelt*." And to each child he gave shiny coins, each according to his or her age. And to the mama, he gave his blessing.

The next morning, when the family awoke, the stranger was gone. The children counted again and again their Hanukkah *gelt,* feeling happier than they had in a long time. The mama went to the flour barrel, thinking how she had only a few cupfuls left for a meager loaf of bread. But when she lifted the cover, to her surprise, she found it full. And mixed in the flour she also found some gold coins. When the mama went to see how many potatoes she had left for the *latke-kugel* for the next three nights of Hanukkah, she discovered bags overflowing with potatoes.

The mama laughed gently as she said, almost to herself, "Our guest must have been Elijah the Prophet."

All day long the younger children played in the snow, and the older ones went sliding and skating on the frozen river. The stranger, who was Elijah the Prophet, saw all of this, smiled, and laughed good-naturedly, his eyes twinkling all the while.

That night, the mama and the children prepared six halves of potatoes and the *shammash,* poured the oil carefully into each scooped-out center, placed a wick into each, and then lighting the *shammash,* they sang the blessings joyfully. On this night, and on all the other nights of Hanukkah, they enjoyed eating their mama's wonderful and more plentiful *latke-kugel* while they watched with pride the flickering lights of their precious potato menorah.

A Menorah in the White House

Eric A. Kimmel

No Jewish person has yet been elected president of the United States. However, there is a menorah in the White House. How it came to be there makes an interesting story.

In 1992, President George W. Bush proclaimed 1993 as the Year of American Craft. Its purpose was to honor the thousands of American craft artists who work in a wide variety of materials: metal, clay, wood, fiber, and glass.

When President William J. Clinton took office in January of 1993, he and First Lady Hillary Rodham Clinton decided to make the White House a showcase for American craft art. Seventy-two of America's best-known craft artists were invited to donate works to a permanent collection. These pieces would be displayed in the White House's formal rooms. This was the beginning of the official White House Collection of American Crafts, an ongoing exhibit of the highest achievements in American craft art.

Zachary Oxman, a Maryland sculptor, was one of the artists invited to participate. He contributed a unique bronze menorah, which he called *A Festival of Light*. Oxman's sculpture shows five young men in formal tuxedos dancing together, holding high the

Hanukkah candles. The collection's catalogue describes the work as "a joyous commemoration of this festival of lights."

Mrs. Clinton hoped to have the menorah in the White House for the 1995 holiday season. The problem was that it was touring museums around the country as part of the crafts collection. Rather than remove it from the exhibit, Mrs. Clinton asked Oxman to sculpt a second menorah. *A Festival of Light II* depicts an even more exciting dance. The two end dancers leave the ground entirely, while the middle figure, holding the *shammash* candle high, leaps in the air with his legs behind him, as if he were taking flight. This menorah was actually lit as part of the White House ceremony marking the beginning of Hanukkah 1995.

When President Clinton's term of office ends, the Oxman menorah will become part of the permanent collection of the Clinton Library.

Rules for Lighting the Hanukkah Lamp

Eric A. Kimmel

Specific rules govern the lighting of the Hanukkah lamp. These rules are taken from the Shulchan Aruch, *a sixteenth-century encyclopedia of Jewish practice.*

A Hanukkah lamp should be beautiful. Purchase the finest one you can afford.

The eight candles should be in a straight row. No candle should be higher than another, since no day of Hanukkah is superior to any other day. Only the ninth candle, the *shammash,* which lights and guards the others, can stand above them.

The Hanukkah candles must burn for at least half an hour. If oil is used, be sure each lamp is filled sufficiently.

Any material that burns may serve as fuel for the Hanukkah lamp and any material may be used for wicks. Oil is preferable to candles. Any oil may be used, but olive oil is best.

A Hanukkah lamp must not be hidden from view. It should be set by a window or in a place where it can be seen from outside.

Hanukkah candles are holy and must not be used for any other purpose. One may not kindle one candle with another, nor is it permitted to use the Hanukkah lights for illumination.

The Hanukkah lamp may be lit at any time between sunset and the time the streets are empty, or until one member of the family goes to bed.

Candles are placed in the Hanukkah lamp from right to left, but they are kindled from left to right. The first candle or wick on the left is lit first.

Hanukkah lights may not be extinguished. They must be permitted to burn out by themselves.

Even if a family is destitute and living on charity, they should not hesitate to pawn their clothes or borrow money to provide oil and lamps for Hanukkah. If one must choose between buying oil for the Hanukkah lamp and wine for the Sabbath, it is better to buy oil.

Hanukkah candles are always kindled before Sabbath candles. Once the Sabbath candles are lit, no other lamps may be lighted until the Sabbath is over. If one cannot afford to buy both Hanukkah candles and Sabbath candles, it is better to buy Hanukkah candles.

Make Your Own Menorah

Judi Lutsky

Driftwood Menorah

If you live near the ocean, you and your family can go to the beach to look for an interesting piece of driftwood. Ask an adult to drill nine holes into the wood. The holes should be large enough to hold Hanukkah candles securely. Line each hole with a small piece of aluminum foil to prevent the wood from being scorched. Be sure to set the hole for the *shammash,* or "helper," candle slightly apart or higher than the others.

Metal Nut Menorah

Sand, paint, and decorate a twelve-inch length of wood. You may use any kind. Plywood works well. Select ten or eleven metal nuts from the hardware store. The nuts should be large enough so that a Hanukkah candle will fit inside each. Bond the metal to the wood with strong glue. Stack and glue two or three nuts on top of each other to hold the *shammash* candle.

Bean Menorah

This is an interesting, decorative project for younger children. Use a piece of colorfully painted cardboard or posterboard. Draw the outline of a menorah. Glue beans onto the shape. Use different kinds of beans for interesting colors and textures.

Blessing the Hanukkah Lights

The candles are placed in the Hanukkah lamp from right to left, but they are always lit from left to right. Light the *shammash* candle first. You will use it to light the others. As you hold the candle in your hand, say these blessings in Hebrew, English, or both:

בָּרוּךְ אַתָּה יי, אֱלוֹהֵינוּ מֶלֶךְ הָעוֹלָם, אֲשֶׁר קִדְּשָׁנוּ בְּמִצְוֹתָיו וְצִוָּנוּ לְהַדְלִיק נֵר שֶׁל חֲנֻכָּה.

Barukh Ata Adonai, Eloheynu Melekh ha'olam, asher kidushanu b'mitzvotav, v'tzivanu l'hadlik ner shel Hanukkah.

(Praised are You, Lord, Our God, Ruler of Creation,
Who has made us holy through His commandments,
and commanded us to kindle the Hanukkah lights.)

בָּרוּךְ אַתָּה יי, אֱלוֹהֵינוּ מֶלֶךְ הָעוֹלָם, שֶׁעָשָׂה נִסִּים לַאֲבוֹתֵינוּ בַּיָּמִים הָהֵם בַּזְּמַן הַזֶּה.

Barukh Ata Adonai, Eloheynu Melekh ha'olam, she'asa nisim l'avoteynu, ba'yamim ha'haym ba'zman hazeh.

(Praised are You, Lord, Our God, Ruler of Creation, Who worked miracles for our ancestors during times past at this season.)

An extra blessing is said on the first night of Hanukkah:

בָּרוּךְ אַתָּה יי, אֱלוֹהֵינוּ מֶלֶךְ הָעוֹלָם, שֶׁהֶחֱיָנוּ, וְקִיְּמָנוּ,
וְהִגִּיעָנוּ לַזְּמַן הַזֶּה.

Barukh Ata Adonai, Eloheynu Melekh ha'olam, she'hekhianu,
v'kiyimanu, v'higiyanu la'zman hazeh.

(Praised are You, Lord, Our God, Ruler of Creation,
Who has strengthened us, supported us, and helped us
to arrive at this season.)

Light the first candle on the left, followed by the one to its right. Continue in this manner until all the candles are lit. After lighting the first candle, sing or recite "Hanerot Hallu":

"We light these candles in memory of the miracles, the remarkable events, the redemptions, and the victories which You granted our forefathers in days past through Your holy priests. Throughout the eight days of Hanukkah, these lights are holy. We must not use them for everyday tasks. We may only look at them, so that we may be reminded to offer thanks and praise to Your glorious Name for Your miracles, Your wonders, and Your deliverance."

The ceremony for lighting the Hanukkah candles concludes with the hymn "Maoz Tzur" (see next page).

Maoz Tzur

Lyrics (Hebrew) by Mordechai*   Music by Debbie Friedman

English lyrics (adapted from a German Hanukkah hymn by Leopold Stein) by Marcus Jastrow and Gustav Gottheil

1. Ma - oz____ tzur____ y' - shu - a - ti____ l' - cha____
2. Rock____ of a - ges,____ let____ our____ song____ praise____

____ na - eh____ l' - sha - bei - - - ach;____
____ Thy____ sav - ing____ pow - - er;____

ti - kon beit____ t' - fi - la - ti____ v' - sham____
Thou____ a - midst____ the____ rag - ing____ foes____ were____

____ to - da____ n' - za - bei - ach.____ L' -
____ our shel - ter - ing tow - er.____

eit ta - chin mat' - bei - ach____ mi -
Fur - ious they as - sailed us____

*The Hanukkah hymn "Maoz Tzur" was written in the thirteenth century by a poet named Mordechai. Nothing else is known about him.

Maoz tzur y'shuati l'cha naeh l'shabeiach;

tikon beit t'filati v'sham toda n'zabeiach.

L'eit tachin mat'beiach mitzar ham'nabeiach,

az eg'mor b'shir miz'mor chanukat hamiz'beiach.

 Rock of ages, let our song praise Thy saving power;

 Thou amidst the raging foes were our sheltering tower.

 Furious they assailed us when Thine arm availed us,

 And Thy word broke their sword, when our own strength failed us.

(Repeat Hebrew verse)

Maoz Tzur!

The Hanukkah Table

Eric A. Kimmel

Feasting is such an important part of Hanukkah that the rabbis banned all fasting during the holiday.

Foods fried in oil are always popular at the Hanukkah table. This is because of their obvious connection with the legend of the miraculous flask of oil that burned for eight days.

Potato pancakes, or latkes, fried golden-brown and served hot with sour cream or applesauce, are to Hanukkah what turkey and pumpkin pie are to Thanksgiving. The word *latke* itself comes from the Greek word *elaion,* meaning olive oil. Latkes, however, are hardly ever cooked in olive oil. The Ashkenazic Jews of Central and Eastern Europe fried their latkes in *shmaltz,* rendered goose or chicken fat. Some people still maintain that frying in *shmaltz* is the only way to prepare "real" latkes.

Not everyone in the Jewish world celebrates Hanukkah with latkes. Latkes were eaten in places like Germany, Russia, and Poland, where potatoes formed a major part of the diet. Further to the south, in Italy, the Balkans, North Africa, and the Middle East, Sephardic Jews preferred sweeter dishes, such as fritters and various kinds of doughnuts. *Sufganiyot*—jelly doughnuts—are the Sephardic equivalent of latkes.

50

Sufganiyot belong to an ancient family of sweet, spongy doughnuts or cookies called *sufgan*. The name comes from a Greek word meaning "puffy and fried." Doughnuts and cookies of this type are popular throughout the Middle East, where they are known by different names: *zvingous, bimuelos, loukoumades*. An interesting legend about the origin of the *sufganiyah* comes from the ancient city of Bukhara, in Central Asia, where Jews have lived for thousands of years.

According to the story, God gave the first *sufganiyah* to Adam and Eve when they left the Garden of Eden to console them for the loss of Paradise. The word *sufganiyah* comes from three Hebrew words meaning, "The end (*sof*) of the garden (*gan*) of God (*Yah*)." The Bukharans also believe the *sufganiyah*'s shape teaches valuable lessons about life. It is round like the wheel of fortune, meaning that someone who is "on the bottom" today may be "on top" tomorrow. The inside is sweet while the outside is plain. This teaches us not to judge others by appearances. Finally, no two *sufganiyot* ever taste alike. You never know what you are getting until you take a bite. That is how life should be lived. Don't try to predict the future. No one knows what tomorrow brings until it arrives.

Dairy foods, especially various kinds of cheeses, have also been associated with Hanukkah for centuries. The custom goes back to the legend of Judith. Eating latkes with sour cream commemorates that event, as does eating cheesecake. Cheesecakes are a traditional Hanukkah dessert. So are cheese-filled cookies called *rugelach*, which come in endless varieties.

The Legend of Judith

The Legend of Judith has long been associated with Hanukkah, even though the events of the story take place long before the time of the Maccabees. The figure of Judith standing with Holofernes's head at her feet was a popular menorah decoration during the eighteenth and nineteenth centuries. Judith served cheese dishes and pancakes with sour cream to Holofernes. That is one of the traditional reasons why these foods are served at Hanukkah time today.

The king of Assyria raised a mighty army to attack Judea. The narrow mountain passes leading to Jerusalem were guarded by the city of Bethulia. Bethulia had to be taken. Otherwise, the invasion would fail.

Holofernes, the Assyrian commander, prepared to besiege Bethulia. His officers warned him that capturing the city would be difficult. The God of Israel was a powerful God. He would surely protect His people if they kept faith with Him.

The Assyrians surrounded the walls of Bethulia. No one could leave or enter. Supplies of food began running low. One day the Assyrians discovered the hidden spring that brought water to the town. They cut it off. Within days, the only water remaining in

Bethulia was what little the people had stored in jugs and cisterns. Resistance seemed hopeless. Faced with starvation and thirst, the people of Bethulia approached Uzziah, the mayor, urging him to surrender to the Assyrians.

"Let us wait five days," Uzziah said. "If God does not send help in that time, I will open the gates."

Among the citizens of Bethulia was a young widow named Judith. She was a woman of great wealth and beauty, respected throughout the city for her piety and charitable works. Judith also approached Uzziah, saying, "It is not proper to put God to a test. If He means to save us, He will do it, whether in five days or five hundred. It is our duty to keep faith that deliverance will come. We must continue to resist the enemy, as long as we can."

"How can we resist?" Uzziah asked. "Our food is running low. We have hardly any water. People are already dying of thirst. In five days there will nothing left to drink in the city. God is our only hope. Pray for rain, Judith. If God does not send rain to fill up our cisterns, I will have no choice but to surrender."

"I will do more than pray," said Judith. "I have a secret plan to save our city. If it succeeds, God will deliver Holofernes into my hands. Tonight, when darkness comes, will you open the gate for me and my servant? I may not tell you more than that."

"May God protect you," Uzziah said. "Whatever you ask will be done."

Judith spent the rest of that day in prayer. When evening came, she put on her finest garments, perfumed her hair, and adorned herself with exquisite jewelry. Then she and her maidservant wrapped themselves in black cloaks. They walked through Bethulia's darkened streets to the city gate. Uzziah met them there. As he opened the gate for Judith, he blessed her with these words: "May God protect you. May you find favor in the eyes of all you meet. May your courage bring deliverance to our people."

Judith and her maidservant slipped out of Bethulia. They followed the rocky trail down the mountainside to the Assyrian camp. A voice rang out. "Halt! Who goes there?"

Judith answered. "I am a Judean, a citizen of Bethulia. I have an important message for your commander."

Soldiers brought word to Holofernes that a beautiful woman had come into the camp, asking to speak with him. Intrigued, he ordered them to bring her to his tent. Judith entered. She bowed before the Assyrian.

When Holofernes asked why she had come, she replied, "My Lord, my maidservant and I have escaped from the besieged city. There is no water left. Soon all the food will be gone as well. I do not want to die, either by thirst, hunger, or by the sword. I have valuable information that will allow you to capture Bethulia without losing a man. Will you promise to spare my life and the lives of my friends if I share it with you?"

Holofernes readily agreed.

Judith continued. "Bethulia will never fall as long as the God of Israel defends it. Within a few days, starvation will force the people to eat forbidden food. In their hunger they will consume cats, dogs, rats, mice, and insects. God will turn away from them because they will have violated His law. He will deliver the city into your hands, and you will overcome it."

"How will I know when this moment comes?" Holofernes asked.

"I have friends within the city. Some of them stand guard on the gate. If you will allow me to come and go as I please, I will approach the walls of Bethulia every night. My friends will signal to me when the Judeans have eaten forbidden food. That is the moment you must attack."

Judith's beauty and her persuasive arguments won over the Assyrian commander. Holofernes readily believed that the God of Israel was as cruel and selfish as the gods of Assyria. He gave Judith and her maidservant a pass that would allow them to go through the Assyrian lines. For the next three nights, Judith and her maid walked to the walls of Bethulia. There, hidden in the shadows, they prayed to God for deliverance.

On the fourth day Holofernes gave a banquet for his officers. He invited Judith to come, for he was smitten by her beauty and wished to feast his eyes upon her. Judith arrived, accompanied by her maid. The two women carried a large hamper filled with food and jugs of wine.

"My Lord Holofernes," said Judith, "I have heard that the wines

of Assyria are the finest in the world. Before you drink, may I offer you one of the wines of Judea. It is an old vintage, very rare. I brought a jug with me when I left the city. You will do me great honor by tasting it."

"It is a small favor to ask," said Holofernes. He held out his goblet. "I will sample this wine. If it is as good as you say, I will have more."

Judith's maidservant filled the commander's cup. He drank. "By the gods of Assyria, this is the best wine I ever tasted!" Holofernes exclaimed. He held out his cup again. Again it was filled, and again he drank. Judith took some cheeses out of the hamper and set them on the banquet table. The salty cheese increased Holofernes's thirst, so he drank some more.

Holofernes greatly enjoyed the food, the wine, and Judith's company. The greedy commander was unwilling to share. He dismissed his officers so he could have the beautiful young woman and her splendid feast all to himself.

"If it pleases my lord, I would be honored to cook some pancakes," Judith said. Holofernes was eager to try this dish. Judith served the pancakes to him, piping hot, heaped with sour cream. Holofernes ate so quickly he burned his tongue. He drank more wine. Then he ate more pancakes. Holofernes ate and drank until all the food was gone and the wine jug was empty. Holofernes stretched out on his couch. Soon he was snoring in a drunk, senseless slumber.

Judith waited quietly until she was sure they were alone and that Holofernes was sound asleep. She reached up and took down Holofernes's sword, which was hanging on the wall. Raising it above her head, she prayed, "God of Israel, give me strength. Deliver Your people from their oppressor."

Judith swung the sword. She severed Holofernes's head from his body with one blow.

Judith lifted the head from the floor and concealed it under her cloak. Then she and her maid left the tent together. They walked through the Assyrian lines. No one challenged them. The soldiers had grown accustomed to seeing both women come and go as they pleased.

Judith and her maid did not stop until they reached the walls of Bethulia. "Open the gate!" she cried to the guards within. "Open quickly! Deliverance is near!"

The soldiers opened the gate. They sent word to Uzziah and the elders of the city that Judith had returned.

"What news do you bring?" Uzziah asked, coming to meet her.

"Give thanks to God! Our city is saved!" Judith said as she pulled out the head of Holofernes.

The gates of Bethulia swung open at dawn. An armed force charged out. When the Assyrians saw the Judeans attacking, they cried for Holofernes, their commander. To their horror, they found his headless corpse lying on the floor of his tent. His head hung from the walls of Bethulia.

Courage deserted the Assyrians. They fled, pursued by the Judeans. Not one in a hundred returned alive to his home.

Thus was the city of Bethulia and the land of Judea saved from a ruthless enemy by the courage of one heroic woman.

May Judith's name live forever!

Judah Maccabee's
Secret Applesauce Recipe

Judi Lutsky

(Adult Supervision Required)

1. Use one pound of apples for each cup of applesauce. Choose any kind of apple.

2. Cut each apple into four pieces. Place the pieces in a big pan (skin and seeds included).

3. Cook over medium heat until the apples are squishy. Stir often. Add a little water if the mixture gets dry or the apples are sticking to the pan.

4. After the apples turn soft and squishy, put them through a food mill until they are smooth.

5. Taste. You may add honey for extra sweetness. A little lemon juice brings out the flavor. Sprinkle with cinnamon and nutmeg. Great on latkes!

Judith's Recipe for Applesauce

Recommended by Holofernes

(Adult Supervision Required)

1. Choose apples with red skins. (One pound of apples for each cup of applesauce.)

2. Cut and core the apples, removing the seeds. Leave the skins on.

3. Put the apples in a large pot and cook over low heat. Cover the pot, but stir the apples often so the mixture does not stick. Do not add water.

4. When the apples are soft and squishy, add ¼ teaspoon each of cloves, nutmeg, and cinnamon.

5. Continue cooking until the mixture bubbles and the juice has evaporated. It usually takes about 45 minutes.

6. Put the mixture through a strainer or food mill.

7. Put it on latkes or eat it by itself. Hold on to your head!

Kartoffel Latkes

Ashkenazic Potato Pancakes
Makes about 24 medium pancakes

(Adult Supervision Required)

8 medium russet potatoes (about 2 pounds), peeled
1 medium yellow onion, finely chopped (about $\frac{1}{2}$ cup)
2 large eggs, lightly beaten
About 3 tablespoons matzoh meal or all-purpose flour
About 1 teaspoon salt
$\frac{1}{4}$ teaspoon ground black pepper
Vegetable oil for frying

1. Grate the potatoes, coarsely or finely, into a bowl of lightly salted water. (The salty water removes the starch and keeps the potatoes from darkening.) Drain and press out the moisture. Stir in the onion, eggs, matzoh meal or flour, salt, and pepper.

2. Heat about $\frac{1}{4}$ inch oil in a large skillet over medium-high heat to about 360 degrees.

3. In batches, drop the batter by heaping tablespoonfuls (or $\frac{1}{3}$ cupfuls) into the oil and flatten with the back of the spoon. Fry until golden brown on both sides, 3 to 5 minutes per side.

4. Drain on paper towels. (The latkes can be kept warm by placing in a single layer on a baking sheet in a 200-degree oven.) Serve with applesauce, jam, or sour cream.

Bimuelos*/Ponchiks

Doughnuts
Makes about 24 medium or 48 small doughnuts

(Adult Supervision Required)

Yeast doughnuts—called *lokmas* in Turkey, *loukoumades* in Greece, and *ponchiks* in Poland—are an ancient form of pastry, prepared in much the same way today as they were two thousand years ago. Fried doughs have been common fare in the Mediterranean region since at least 2,500 years ago. The trick to making nongreasy fritters is the temperature of the oil. If the oil is not hot enough, the dough will absorb it. If the oil is too hot, the outsides of the dough will brown before the insides have cooked.

*The word "bimuelos" is Ladino, a dialect of Spanish spoken by the descendants of Jews exiled from Spain in 1492.

1 package (2½ teaspoons) active dry yeast

2 cups warm water (105 to 110 degrees for dry yeast, 80 to 85 degrees
   for fresh yeast)

1 teaspoon sugar or honey

2½ cups all-purpose flour

⅛ teaspoon salt

Vegetable oil for deep-frying

1 recipe of sugar syrup (see below) cooled, or confectioners' sugar
   for dusting

1. Dissolve the yeast in ¼ cup of the water. Stir in the sugar or honey and let stand until foamy, 5 to 10 minutes.

2. Combine the flour and salt in a large bowl and make a well in the center. Pour the yeast mixture and remaining water into the well and stir until smooth. The dough will not be very thick. Cover and let rise at room temperature until double in bulk, about 1½ hours. Stir.

3. Heat 2 inches of oil over a medium heat to 375 degrees.

4. Dip a teaspoon or tablespoon into cold water and use the spoon to drop the dough into the hot oil. In batches, deep-fry the doughnuts until golden brown on all sides, about 3 minutes. Drain on paper towels.

5. Dip the warm doughnuts into the cooled syrup or sprinkle with confectioners' sugar. Serve immediately. (To serve *bimuelos* later, let them cool without the syrup or sugar and store in an airtight container. Just before serving, dip into warm syrup.)

Variation:

Zelebi (Middle Eastern funnel cakes): Drop the dough from a large spoon or squeeze it from a plastic squeeze bottle into the hot oil in a spiral fashion, forming a 6-inch-long coil. Makes about 26 cakes. (This pastry, popular from the Maghreb to India, is called *chebbakiah/zangulas* in Morocco, *zinghol* in Syria, *zalabia* in Iraq, and *jalebi* in India.)

Sugar Syrup
Makes about $1\frac{1}{2}$ cups

2 cups sugar (or 1 cup sugar and 1 cup honey)
1 cup water
2 teaspoons lemon juice

1. Combine all of the ingredients in a heavy 1-quart saucepan.
2. Bring to a boil, stirring frequently. Reduce the heat to medium-low and simmer, without stirring, until the mixture is syrupy or registers 212 degrees on a candy thermometer, about 10 minutes.
3. Let cool. Store in the refrigerator.

Variations:

Cinnamon Syrup: Add 1 cinnamon stick or ½ teaspoon ground cinnamon.

Orange Syrup: Just before removing the syrup from the heat, stir in 1 tablespoon orange blossom water. Or add 1 tablespoon grated orange zest with the sugar.

Rose Syrup: Just before removing the syrup from the heat, stir in 1 tablespoon rose water.

Two More
Hanukkah Treats

Judi Lutsky

Hanukkah Gelt Mix

(Adult Supervision Suggested)

This healthy treat is easy to make, and it's great for Hanukkah party favors.

1 bag chocolate or carob chips
1 bag shredded coconut
1 box seedless golden raisins
1 pound of nuts (unsalted peanuts, almonds, cashews—your choice)

Mix the ingredients together in a large bowl. Spoon into plastic sandwich bags and tie with bright ribbon or yarn.

Hanukkah Cookies

(Adult Supervision Required)

$\frac{1}{2}$ cup butter or margarine

$\frac{1}{2}$ cup white sugar

2 tablespoons milk or cream

$\frac{1}{2}$ teaspoon baking soda

$\frac{1}{2}$ teaspoon vanilla

1 egg

1 pinch of salt

2 cups flour

1. Mix the ingredients together in a large bowl to form a stiff dough. (Young bakers enjoy doing this with their hands. Make sure they are washed thoroughly first.)

2. Refrigerate the cookie dough overnight.

3. On baking day, roll out the dough on a floured surface until it is $\frac{1}{4}$-inch thick. Cut out cookie shapes with cookie cutters. Sprinkle the cookies with powdered sugar or top with frosting.

4. Place on a greased cookie sheet and bake at 375 degrees for 10 to 12 minutes.

(Cookie cutters with Hanukkah shapes—menorahs, dreidels, Stars of David—can be found in most synagogue gift shops.)

Hanukkah in Alaska

Barbara Brown

In Alaska, in the winter, you have to watch out for moose. You have to look both ways when you go out the front door, making sure there are no moose around. And when my mother drives me places, she drives slowly, looking out for moose. Sometimes, when we're skiing, a moose will come out on the trail, maybe even with a calf. Then we all have to ski around them in the deep snow. And at school, when we're all playing outside and a moose comes up, then we have to hug a tree. A moose can't step on you or knock you over if you're hugging a tree.

Also, during the winter in Alaska, it's dark. Not just at night for sleeping, but almost all the time. It doesn't get light till it's already snack time at school, and it's dark again practically right after lunch and class meeting. Daytime is only five hours long. And sometimes, it seems even darker than that, like when the snow covers up the windows.

I don't think the snow would cover up the windows all by itself, even though Alaskan snow never melts in between snows. It just gets deeper and deeper. Still, I don't think it would cover the windows if it weren't for the snow from the roof. In the winter, my father has to climb up on the roof and shovel the snow off to make sure the roof doesn't cave in. Snow piles up everywhere.

So that's why a moose lives in our backyard. The snow is too deep for her to walk around on her skinny legs. And she's hungry. So she just stops in our yard and eats our trees away. I try throwing carrots to her, even cookies, but she just really likes the tree with my swing on it. Once, we saw a moose walking around town with a whole swing set in his antlers! He'd gotten tangled and just tore the whole swing set away. I'm worried about my blue swing. I wish that moose would get out of our yard.

I think the dark and that moose are making me kind of grumpy, because even Hanukkah hasn't cheered me up. My friends and I play spinning dreidels in the snow, and every time the mail lady comes, she has another present for me from my aunts and uncles Outside. (Do you know that everywhere else from Alaska is called "Outside"?) But every time I light a new candle, I look out the window and it's still dark, and that moose is still there. My mother and I threw some apples, but she just watched them fall while she ate more tree.

Just as I was lighting the last Hanukkah candle, my father said, "Let's go outside. I have something to show you."

"With the moose there?"

"Don't worry, we'll stay far away."

So I put on my long underwear and two layers of socks. I put on my thick, baggy pants and a sweatshirt. I put a snowsuit on over all that, two layers of mittens and a hat. Still, it's freezing cold outside, and it's very dark, and I do not like being anywhere near that moose. I want that moose away from my swing!

"Dad, what are we waiting for?"

"Just wait, you'll see." But he's looking at the sky.

I'm looking at that moose. Mom says, "Maybe we can try some spinach leaves. Maybe she'll leave your swing alone for some green leaves."

But the spinach doesn't work, and I'm awfully cold. Dad is still looking at the sky. Mom thinks maybe she'll try a hard-boiled egg for the moose, but it just rolls on the snow till neither the moose nor we can even see it. I am freezing.

Suddenly, Dad points up in the sky. There are pink and purple and orange ribbons of light! The sky is full of color, all swirling and

shining and glowing. Against the dark black of the sky, the lights are bright and beautiful. I have never seen anything like this. So much light, and so big. Filling the sky, coloring the sky. A rainbow on black velvet.

"They're called the Northern Lights," my father says. "Aurora borealis. They happen especially up here in Alaska. Our very own Hanukkah Festival of Lights."

Like ribbons of wax, all the candles from all the menorahs, melting into the dark, lighting it up. I stare at those lights. I stare so hard, I don't even notice the moose sticking her head through my swing. But my mother does. Next thing I know, the moose is yanking on the chain, pulling on the whole tree. I hear creaks and clanks, snorts and scuffing. I can't stand it. That moose will tear everything up.

But then I see my mother, running from the house, right near the moose. She lays something down on the snow, AND THE MOOSE SNIFFS, turns her head. My mother backs up, lays another down. The moose stretches her head, reaches for it. My mother keeps backing up, laying them down, and the moose follows her! Out the yard, across the street, AWAY! I'm so happy, I could cheer—but I don't want to attract that moose back again.

I look at the sky, at the lights. I'm so happy to see those lights. I'm so happy that moose is gone. "Mom," I ask, "what did you feed her? What did she like so much?"

"Latkes," she answered.

Hanukkah can be pretty funny in Alaska, and God can make miracles in a lot of different ways.

Dreidels

Eric A. Kimmel

What is a dreidel?

A dreidel is a four-sided top used during the eight-day celebration of Hanukkah. The Hebrew word for dreidel is *sivivon*.

What are the four letters on its sides? What do they mean?

The four Hebrew letters are נ (*nun*), ג (*gimel*), ה (*hey*), and ש (*shin*). They stand for the words נס (*nes*) גדול (*gadol*) היה (*haya*) שם (*sham*), meaning: "A great miracle happened there." Dreidels used in Israel substitute the letter פ (*peh*) for the letter *shin*. The letters *nun*, *gimel*, *hey*, *peh* stand for the words נס (*nes*) גדול (*gadol*) היה (*haya*) פה (*poh*)—"A great miracle happened here." This makes sense, since Israel is where the miracle took place.

What miracle was that?

The "great miracle" refers to the small jar of oil that burned for eight days. The words also honor the victory won by the Maccabees, who defeated a professional Greek army that outnumbered them four to one.

How do you play the dreidel game?

It's easy. You can play with pennies, nuts, candy, or whatever you'd like. Let's play with pennies. We divide the pennies equally among the number of players. Each player puts a penny into the pot. The first player spins. The dreidel falls on נ (*nun*). For the purposes of the dreidel game, *nun* means "nothing." Nothing happens. Everyone puts another penny into the pot, and the first player passes the dreidel to the person on the left.

The second player spins. The dreidel falls on ש (*shin*). *Shin* means "put." The second player puts in a penny. Everyone, including the second player, puts another penny into the pot and the dreidel passes to the third player.

The third player spins. The dreidel falls on ה (*hey*). *Hey* means "half." The player takes half the pennies in the pot. Then everyone puts in a penny, and the dreidel passes to the fourth player.

The fourth player spins. This time the dreidel falls on ג (*gimel*), the winning letter. *Gimel* means "all." The fourth player takes the whole pot. Everyone puts in a penny and the game goes on.

The game continues until one person wins all the pennies.

Can you play dreidel on a computer?

Yes! A shareware dreidel program for Macintosh computers does exist. It's called DreidelLand. It was created by Jacob Berry of San Francisco for his own children. You can send an e-mail message to dundaware@aol.com for more information. Other programs may be available, too. Check the internet.

Did the Maccabees play with dreidels?

No. The earliest reference to a dreidel occurs hundreds of years after the time of the Maccabees.

Who invented the dreidel?

No one knows for sure. One account traces the dreidel back to the Bar Kokhba revolution against the Romans in 135 C.E. After putting down the rebellion, the Roman emperor Hadrian outlawed the Jewish religion. Jews were forbidden to study the Torah. Those caught violating the decree were put to death.

Hadrian's persecution failed. Jews continued to worship and study more than ever. They studied the Torah in attics, cellars, and caves. When a lookout warned that Roman soldiers were approaching, the Jews hid the scrolls. All the Romans found when they entered the hiding place were a group of people playing a gambling game with a child's top. Religious Jews did not gamble, so these people could not possibly be studying the Torah. Or so the Romans thought.

It may have been at this time that the four letters came to be written on the dreidel's sides. The words they represented reminded people that just as God had freed their ancestors from a tyrant in days gone by, so too would He overthrow the present tyrant in days to come.

The hope and courage embodied in the humble dreidel have sustained the Jewish people throughout the ages. Indeed, Hadrian is dust and the mighty Roman Empire only a memory. But dreidels still spin at Hanukkah time.

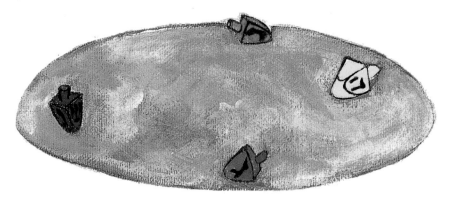

Dreidel Rhyme

J. Patrick Lewis

Dreidel, dreidel, what's to eat?
Show me something *very* sweet!

Put one candy in the middle,
Spin the dreidel just a little—

If the dreidel comes up *shin* ש
Put one piece of candy in.

If it's half—the letter *hey* ה —
Take one half the pot away.

If the *gimel* ג should appear,
You win everything, my dear!

But if *nun* נ should show its face,
Someone else spins in your place.

Now before we spin again,
Put another candy in.

Dreidel, dreidel, what's to eat?
Show me something *very* sweet!

Dreidel Variations

Eric A. Kimmel

Once you know how to play dreidel, it is easy to invent variations on the game. Here are some that are fun to try.

Gematria

This game is based on the fact that the letters of the Hebrew alphabet also function as numbers.

ג = 3

ה = 5

נ = 50

ש = 300

As the players spin the dreidel, they add up the numbers each letter is worth. The first player to reach 1,000 wins.

Dueling Dreidels

Draw a circle about six inches in diameter on a piece of paper or cardboard. Every player has a dreidel. They put their dreidels in the circle and spin them at once. The last dreidel left spinning inside the circle wins.

Dreidel Marathon

You need a stopwatch to play this game. The players take turns spinning their dreidels. Time each spin with a stopwatch. Keep track of how long each spin lasts. The players add up their spins. The first to accumulate 100 seconds wins.

Crazy Shin

This is played like the basic dreidel game, except the player whose dreidel shows the letter *shin* has to do something silly: bark like a dog; sing a song; tell a joke; wear a funny hat. Players decide this in advance. Don't make it too silly. *You* may have to do it.

Wild Nun

Nun is the letter to avoid. If the dreidel lands on this letter, you lose your whole stake and you're out of the game. Your stake goes into the pot, and the game continues until only one player is left.

Right Side Up

Barbara Diamond Goldin

"On Hanukkah we play dreidel, spinning it round and round, hoping it will land on the letter *gimel,*" the rabbi explained. "Then we claim everything in the pot. If it lands on *hey,* that's not such bad luck. We take half. But we groan if it turns up *nun,* nothing, or even worse, *shin,* put one in."

As Inna listened to the rabbi, she thought of how she had played the dreidel game with her father in Russia. Of how her father carved a new one out of wood every year. Of her favorite dreidel, the one with Stars of David circling around a brave Judah the Maccabee. But since coming to America, her parents had been so busy finding them a place to live and working, they hadn't even unpacked the dreidels.

Suddenly, Inna realized the rabbi was still talking. "Our world, too, spins round and round just like a top, a dreidel," he was saying. "And we do not know how our luck will fall. Will we be wealthy or poor? Wise or a fool? Well liked or without a friend? Or perhaps wealthy one day, poor the next. Who knows?

"And there's another way that life is just like our little dreidel." The rabbi lifted up a see-through plastic one, the kind usually filled with chocolate coins. "See this central point on which the dreidel turns?" he asked. "So, too, does life have a central source—the Almighty. We mustn't forget that even as life seems to be spinning and spinning, taking us away with it, who knows where."

While she walked home from the synagogue, Inna remembered what the rabbi said. We've been lucky, and we haven't been lucky, she thought. We're lucky to be in America, in our own apartment, near our friends and relatives. And we don't have to be afraid to say we're Jewish out loud like we were in Russia. Papa doesn't have to smuggle in Bibles or carve our own dreidels in America. Here you see Bibles and dreidels in shop windows and watch Hanukkah shows right on television.

But as far as being wealthy, that dreidel was definitely landing on *nun*s and *shin*s. Where were the jobs in the symphony for Mama, who played the violin, and Papa, who played the flute? Sometimes it seemed as if things had turned upside down for them. In Moscow, Mama and Papa had to work so hard to be Jewish. In America, they had to work so hard just to be musicians. Were Mama and Papa spinning and twirling away, just like the rabbi said?

During the eight days of Hanukkah, Mama no longer had the time to sit Inna and little Leo down to hear the story of brave Judah the Maccabee and how he led the fight for religious freedom long ago. She was teaching every kid in the neighborhood to squeak away on the violin. And for Hanukkah, Papa couldn't carve dreidels with them, big and little, fat and thin, to give to all their cousins. He was teaching every kid on the other side of town to make some decent noises on the flute.

And as the time in America passed, Inna could hardly remember Mama's story about who Judah the Maccabee was or how Papa

carved a dreidel. Leo thought Judah the Maccabee was a Jewish Superman and that all dreidels were pink and blue plastic and came from a store. But as the rabbi said, the world was always spinning in cycles, just like a dreidel, and one could always hope it would turn right side up again for them.

It was just before the first night of Hanukkah, their second in America, when Inna tapped her father on the shoulder as he was about to leave for the music school. "I know you don't have time to carve dreidels with us anymore, Papa," she said. "But couldn't we have a Hanukkah party and invite everyone and spin the ones we made in Moscow and play pennies and give little presents and—"

"Whoa, Inna," Papa interrupted.

"Well, you don't want Leo to think all dreidels are pink and blue plastic and come from a store, do you? Or that Judah the Maccabee was Superman with a bow and arrow and a little hat on top of his head?"

"He thinks that?"

Inna nodded.

Papa laughed, but then he looked serious. "All right, Inna. We can have a party for the first night. After all, a big Hanukkah party was something we could never do in Russia. A party!" He snorted.

"We could never even light the menorah for fear we'd be reported. No, you are right. Mama and I will just cancel all our lessons for the night."

Inna hugged her father and went right to work. She telephoned all her relatives and neighbors to invite them to the party. "Bring a friend, too," she told them.

Then she dragged little Leo down to the basement, carrying the key to the storage closet in her pocket. They found their boxes still tied with rope, with Russian letters printed on the sides. They opened one and then another, looking for the old dreidels. One small box in the back had their Jewish things from Russia. The old prayer book and prayer shawl that belonged to great-grandfather was on top. Waiting underneath were all the wooden dreidels. Even in the dark of the basement, Inna could recognize the designs carved around the *shin*s and *nun*s, *hey*s and *gimel*s, designs carved by Papa and grandpa and great-grandfather. There was her favorite dreidel and others with crowns and lions and birds, spears and elephants.

"Elephants?" asked Leo.

"The Greeks used them to fight Judah and the Maccabees," said Inna. "Mama will tell you the whole story. Promise."

They wrapped all the dreidels in an old scarf and carried them upstairs, big ones and little ones, fat and thin ones—but no pink and blue plastic ones.

On the first night of Hanukkah, Mama and Papa made latkes in the kitchen while Inna and Leo answered the door and welcomed the guests. Once the doorbell started to ring, it didn't stop. There were aunts, uncles, and cousins, neighbors and friends, and friends of friends, too. When Inna and Leo lit the candles in the menorah, everyone sang the blessings. They ate the latkes and twirled the dreidels. And Mama told all about brave Judah and the Maccabees. And the elephants.

Of course, Mama and Papa brought out their violin and flute so they could play the Hanukkah melodies and everyone could sing along. Soon, though, everyone stopped singing to listen to the beautiful music. When Mama and Papa were done, they took a bow, smiles on their faces.

"It is so nice to play for friends and family," Mama said.

Suddenly someone they didn't know, one of the friends of a friend, stood up. "How would you like to play for more people? For an audience of people?" he asked.

Mama and Papa looked puzzled.

"I work for the symphony," he said, "and would like to recommend you two. As a matter of fact, we're auditioning right now. Would you be interested?"

"Interested?" repeated Mama, stunned.

"We would love to," said Papa. "It is what we did in Russia." He turned to smile at Inna who held up the last wooden dreidel that Papa had carved before they came to America, her favorite, with the Stars of David circling around Judah the Maccabee. She held the dreidel right side up, the *gimel* and *hey* turned toward Papa, and smiled happily back.

The Dreidel Song

Music and lyrics by Debbie Friedman

CHORUS

Beginning slowly, then gradually getting faster

Nun, Gi-mel, Hey, Shin, watch the drei-del spin, spin, spin.

Nun, Gi-mel, Hey, Shin, watch now, let the fun be-gin.

Nun, Gi-mel, Hey, Shin, spin the drei-del, try to win___ and

sing a-long our drei-del song with me.

Last Time to Coda

VERSES

1. See the drei - del spin - ning 'round, spin - ning ___ 'round and 'round and 'round;
2. You take no - thing Nun will say; Gi - mel ___ wins, it's fun to play.

when it stops it will tell you, this is what you have to do. ___
Hey takes half, but land on Shin and you'll have to put some in. ___

CODA

Sing a - long our drei - del song with me. ___ Sing a - long our

drei - del song with me. ___

Ever After

Jane Yolen

When I was four
and my brother Stevie brand new,
we lived in Virginia
with Grandma and Grandpa
only one long block from the bay.
My father had sailed off
on a great big ship
to go to war against Hitler.
But what did I know
about war, about Hitler?
All I knew was that Daddy was gone,
gone a long way,
longer than the block,
and we did not know when he'd be home.
"If ever," somebody whispered,
thinking I did not hear.
If ever.

Ever was a long time
longer than it had taken

for Stevie to be born,
longer than it had taken
to move down from New York.
Ever.
Ever after.
And no one said *happy*.
When Chanukah came around
we had presents from Grandpa
and the dreidel spinning:
half for me,
take all,
give to the pot,
nothing
it should have said.
But I thought it read
ever.
Ever after.

Not one side said: *happy*.
I cried for my daddy then
and Grandpa picked me up.
"Look at the candles, Janie."
I looked.
"One a month for a miracle."
He thought to comfort me.
He thought I would forget.
But I marked the months off
one at a time,

till eight were gone
and no miracle.
"Miracle?" asked Grandpa
when he found me sobbing.
He had forgotten
our Chanukah game
so could not stop my tears.
But in the ninth month
Daddy came home,
his arm in a sling.

"A miracle," I cried out
as he swung me up in his good arm,
round and round
like a dreidel spinning.
"We forgot to count the *shamash*."
I knew then as I know now
a miracle truly happened there,
one long block from the bay,
one long year from the war.
gimmel,

shin,

nun,

hey,

round and round,

round and round,

happy

ever

after.

S·o·u·r·c·e N·o·t·e·s

· <u>The Story of the Maccabees</u>   Two excellent sources for understanding the complex history of the Maccabean period are Solomon Zeitlin's *The Rise and Fall of the Judean State* (Philadelphia: Jewish Publication Society of America, 1968) and Menahem Stern's "The Period of the Second Temple" in *A History of the Jewish People,* edited by H. H. Ben-Sasson (Cambridge, Massachusetts: Harvard University Press, 1976).

· <u>From the First Book of Maccabees</u>   The First Book of Maccabees is a Greek translation of a now-lost Hebrew manuscript. Although the original author is unknown, he may have taken part in the events he describes. The First and Second Books of the Maccabees are important sources of information about the Hasmonean period.

· <u>Holy Light, Holy Lamps</u>   God's instructions to Moses concerning the menorah can be found in Exodus 25:31–40. The Stone edition of the Chumash (Brooklyn, New York: Mesorah Publications, Ltd., 1993), edited by Rabbi Nosson Scherman, offers an excellent commentary to the biblical text. The article "Menorah" in the *Encyclopedia Judaica* (New York: Macmillan, 1976) is filled with information about the menorah's subsequent history and symbolism.

· <u>Hanukkah Lamps</u>   Nancy Berman's *The Art of Hanukkah* (New York: Hugh Lauter Levin Associates, 1996) contains a great deal of information about the

Hanukkah lamp, its history and design, as well as outstanding photographs of significant traditional and modern menorahs.

· Rules for Lighting the Hanukkah Lamp   These rules are taken from the *Shulchan Aruch* by Rabbi Joseph Caro, a sixteenth-century writer in Safed (a city in what is now northern Israel). Rabbi Caro's masterful codification still remains the authoritative guide to Jewish law and practice. Two modern sources for information about Hanukkah observance are Rabbi Isaac Klein's *A Guide to Jewish Religious Practice* (New York: Jewish Theological Seminary, 1979) and Abraham Milgrom's *Jewish Worship* (Philadelphia: Jewish Publication Society of America, 1971).

· Blessing the Hanukkah Lights   An excellent presentation of the complete ritual for lighting the Hanukkah candles, as well as a great deal of additional information about the history and spiritual significance of the holiday, can be found in Rabbis Hersh Goldwurm and Meir Zlotowitz's *Chanukah—Its History, Observance, and Significance* (Brooklyn, New York: Mesorah Publications, Ltd., 1996).

· The Hanukkah Table   Rabbi Gil Marks's *The World of Jewish Cooking* (New York: Simon & Schuster, 1996), Gloria Kaufer Green's *The Jewish Holiday Cookbook* (New York: Times Books, 1985), and Joan Nathan's *Jewish Cooking in America* (New York: Alfred A. Knopf, 1995) and *The Jewish Holiday Kitchen* (New York: Schocken Books, 1988) present valuable information about the history and traditions of Jewish cooking, as well as dozens of mouth-watering recipes.

· The Legend of Judith   The story of Judith and Holofernes dates back to the second century B.C.E. Scholars believe it was written during the Maccabean period to inspire resistance to foreign invaders. The original Hebrew manuscript has been lost. The oldest known versions of the story are in Greek.

· Dreidels   Nancy Berman's *The Art of Hanukkah* (New York: Hugh Lauter Levin Associates, 1996) offers interesting information on the history of dreidels and dreidel making, as well as photographs of traditional and modern dreidels.

P·e·r·m·i·s·s·i·o·n·s

"The Blessing" by Peninnah Schram, copyright © 1996. Reprinted with permission.

"Chanukah in Alaska" by Barbara Brown, copyright © 1996. Reprinted with permission.

"The Dreidel Song" reprinted with the permission of Sounds Write Productions, Inc. (ASCAP) from *Miracles and Wonders* by Deborah Lynn Friedman (ASCAP). Music and lyrics by Debbie Friedman. Copyright © 1987 by Deborah Lynn Friedman.

"Ever After" by Jane Yolen reprinted by permission of G.P. Putnam's Sons from *Milk and Honey: A Year of Jewish Holidays,* text copyright © 1996 by Jane Yolen.

"Hanukkah Haiku" by Erica Silverman, copyright © 1996. Reprinted with permission.

"Hanukkah Lights" and "Dreidel Rhyme" by J. Patrick Lewis, copyright © 1996. Reprinted with permission.

"Kartoffel Latkes" and "Bimuelos/Ponchiks" reprinted with the permission of Simon & Schuster from *The World of Jewish Cooking* by Gil Marks. Copyright © 1996 by Gil Marks.

"The Lost Menorah" by Howard Schwartz, copyright © 1983. Reprinted with permission.